D1228396

NATHAN MEETS HIS MONSTERS

Karen,
I hope
you enjoy
getting to
know your
monsters!

Love Kropp

Written by Joseph Kropp, Ph.D.
Illustrated by Philip Johnston

Day to Day Enterprises   *Lake Shore, Maryland*

Book Design: MyLinda Butterworth

ISBN-13:   978-1-890905-59-0 hardcover
ISBN-13:   978-1-890905-58-3 softcover

Printed in the United States of America
10 9 8 7 6 5 4 3 2 1

Dedication

In recognition of Dr. Richard Schwartz, who, by listening carefully to his clients and managing his own monsters, brought beautiful clarity to our understanding of how to help the monsters inside us all.

———

"From their earliest years, children live on familiar terms with disrupting emotions...
Fantasy is the best means they have for taming Wild Things." --Maurice Sendak

Published by Day to Day Enterprises • Lake Shore, Maryland
Visit us on the web at http://www.daytodayenterprises.com

Something woke Nathan up.

He tried to hide under the covers... but he found another surprise!

He wanted to believe his **sister** when she said, "There's no such thing," — but it wasn't easy.

When his Mom and Dad came to check on him, Nathan told them about the monsters in his room.

Nathan's Mom wanted
to take him to the Doctor.
But his father didn't.

But even the
Doctor told
Nathan there was no such thing as
monsters. That didn't help either.

So they took Nathan to a Talking Doctor. She said, "Of course there are monsters. Which one would you like to talk to first?"

"But what if they are here to help you?" she asked.

"If they want to help me, why do they keep scaring me?"

"I don't know...
but I know
who does."

"Who?" asked Nathan.
"They do," said the Talking Doctor.
"If you ask the monsters, they can tell you."

"You could start by taking a deep breath, closing your eyes, and thinking about one of the monsters."

"When I see Closet Monster, it feels funny right here," said Nathan, holding his tummy.

"Let's use that tummy feeling to help you focus on Closet Monster. How do you feel toward him?" asked the Talking Doctor.

"Ask the part of you that doesn't like him to take a rest, just so you can get to know Closet Monster," she said. "We will make sure he doesn't scare you."

This time when the Talking Doctor asked how he felt toward Closet Monster, Nathan said, "I wonder why he keeps scaring me."

"So ask him," she said. "Ask him why he's in your closet scaring you."

"He says when I'm scared, Mom and Dad stop arguing and come see about me," said Nathan.

"So let him know you understand he is really just protecting you from being scared," said the Talking Doctor.

"What do you see now?"

"Little Monste
is on the stairs
listening to Mom and Dad
arguing," said Nathan.

"He looks scared."

"Can you go and be with him?"
said the Talking Doctor.

"I can help him,"
said Nathan.

Then the Talking Doctor asked, "What does he need now?"

"He wants to play with me," said Nathan.

"Is that okay with you?" the Talking Doctor asked.

"I'd like that," replied Nathan.

"He's not scared anymore," said Nathan.

"So when you listen and understand them, Monsters aren't so scary after all," said the Talking Doctor.

"But what if I find other Monsters?" asked Nathan.

"I'll bet you'll know what to do next time," said the Talking Doctor.

His Mom put her arm around him. "We're always here for you, Nathan." Then his Dad smiled and said, "For you and your Monsters."

TO THOSE WHO USE THIS BOOK TO SPEND LOVING TIME WITH A CHILD

This story is based on the Internal Family Systems (IFS) Model and is designed to give Caregivers, Teachers, and Therapists a tool for helping young children identify and unburden their fears. When children learn to listen to them, fears become less extreme and scary. And when children are not hindered by their fears, they become calm and curious rather than fearful; clear, confident, compassionate, and courageous within themselves and with those around them; creative in their approach to life and connected to others in meaningful ways.

When reading this book to children, invite them to voice their own fears and encourage them to listen to those fears, just like Nathan did in the story.

For more information about IFS, go to http://www.selfleadership.org.

ABOUT THE AUTHOR AND ILLUSTRATOR

Joseph Kropp, Ph.D., Licensed Psychologist and Certified IFS Therapist, has worked with children and families for over 30 years. His works have been published in professional books and journals and in Southern Living magazine. He is an award-winning author of children's novels. Nathan Meets His Monsters is his first picture book for children.

Phil Johnston is an Illustrator and Animator residing in Vancouver, BC. After working in television for over 8 years, he chose to direct his creative talents to help big, important ideas reach more people. Phil's proud to have worked with Joe to help share IFS with children and their families.
See more of his work at philwjohnston.com

CPSIA information can be obtained at www.ICGtesting.com
Printed in the USA
LVOW010723171012

303207LV00002B/2/P